Totally Uncool

by Janice Levy
illustrated by Chris Monroe

Totally Uncool

Dad's new girlfriend is weird.
Totally uncool.

She plays the tuba.
Reads poems that don't rhyme.
Falls asleep sitting up.

Dad calls her Sweetie Pie.
I don't call her anything.

She doesn't play football.
Or work out in a gym.
Video games? She hasn't a clue.

Sweetie Pie would never think of ice skating.
Or horseback riding.
Shooting hoops? I don't think so.

She doesn't bake cakes.
Her kitchen floor is too shiny.
Mostly everything she eats is green.

Sweetie Pie wears trainers with skirts.
And sometimes backwards baseball caps.

Her hair is porcupiny.

She sings opera to her goldfish.
Hangs upside down to relax.
Forgets the answers to riddles.

She speaks French to her neighbours.

Baby talk to my dad.

Japanese to her plants.

And mish-mosh to me.

Scary movies give her nightmares.
Cats make her sneeze.
Loud music clogs her ears.

Sweetie Pie is weird. Totally uncool.
Still, out of all the girlfriends,
she's lasted the longest....

She listens to me without the TV on.
Keeps my secrets secret.
Never interrupts me when I stutter.

She tests me on my spelling words.
Lets me slam doors when things aren't fair.
She never calls me stupid.

At school plays, Dad's new girlfriend
claps the loudest.

She waits (and waits) at the finish line.

She helped me with my party costume.
It won First Prize.
Nobody else came as Broccoli.

She doesn't call my stuff "junk."
Or touch it without asking first.
I can make messes if they're just on me.

If I'm grumpy, Dad's new girlfriend
doesn't try to make me laugh.
Or ask a million questions.
She lets me be quiet.

She doesn't shout when I forget things.
Or drop things.
Well, maybe just a little.

She takes my side when I get in a fight.
She rubs away my headaches.
She says it's okay to cry.

She doesn't order me around.
Or make me do things "just because."
She doesn't stay cross forever.

To Rick, with all my love
—*J. L.*

To Mickey
—*C. M.*

Text copyright © 1999 by Janice Levy
Illustrations copyright © 1999 by Chris Monroe

Published by arrangement with
Carolrhoda Books, Inc., a division of Lerner Publishing Group
241 First Avenue North, Minneapolis, MN 55401 U.S.A.

First published in Great Britain in 2001 by
Zero to Ten Limited, 327 High Street, Slough, Berkshire SL1 1TX

A CIP catalogue record for this book is available
from the British Library

ISBN: 1-84089-078-9

Manufactured in the United States of America
1 2 3 4 5 6 - JR - 04 03 02 01 00 99